SO YOU WANT TO SEE THE WORLD?

BY JASON PRUETT

PLAIN SIGHT PUBLISHING
AN IMPRINT OF CEDAR FORT, INC.
SPRINGVILLE, UTAH

ISBN 13: 978-1-4621-2177-9

Published by Plain Sight Publishing, an imprint of Cedar Fort, Inc.
2373 W. 700 S., Springville, UT 84663
Distributed by Cedar Fort, Inc., www.cedarfort.com

Library of Congress Control Number: 2017959442

Cover design and typesetting by Shawnda T. Craig
Cover design © 2018 Cedar Fort, Inc.
Edited by Kathryn Watkins and Kaitlin Barwick

Printed in the United States of America

10 9 8 7 6 5 4 3 2 1

Printed on acid-free paper

You're off on your journey! It's already started.
There are lands to be seen and pictured and charted.
There are oceans to cross, there are islands to visit.
There's life to get living, so go on and **LIVE IT!**

On foot or on boat, on wheels, on wings.
On planes or on trains, on all kinds of things.
You're on the right path as long as you're trying.
There's no time to lose, it's time to **GET FLYING.**

There are rivers to cross and mountains to climb,
And flowers to smell, if you've got the time.
There are views to get viewing, so go on and view them.
There are things to get doing, so go on and **DO THEM.**

From Rome to Australia, Hawaii to Bali,
Vancouver, Brazil, Antarctica, Mali.
YOU'LL CHECK
all the continents, swim all the seas,
And when you're in Florida, you'll stop by the Keys.

YOU'LL SEE seven wonders, and then you'll see more.
All over this world there are wonders galore.

Huge ancient heads, a near-endless wall,
And pyramids over four hundred feet tall.

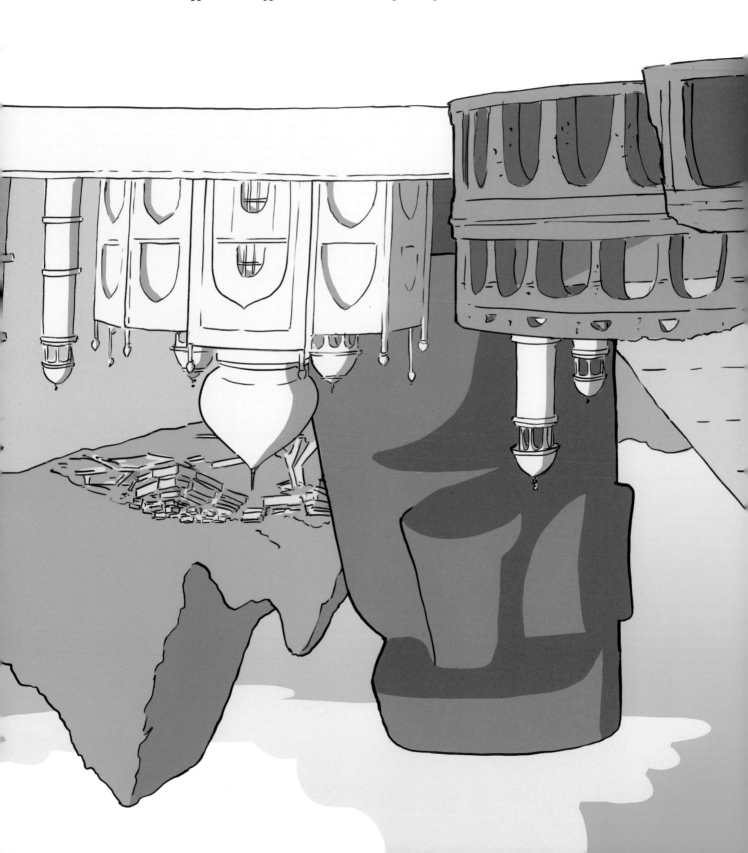

AND OH THE FOOD,

the food you will eat,
From kebabs to "what's that" with mystery meat.
Gelato and sushi and all kinds of rice,
And you have to try insects at least once or twice.

There are some things out there
that'd like to **EAT YOU.**
And some of them don't even bother to chew.
Lions and tigers, mosquitoes and midges,
And six kinds of nasty old trolls under bridges.

You'll be walking the hills, no time for sore feet.

You've got places to go and people to meet.

All over the world, I think you will find,

Most people are generous,

HELPFUL, AND KIND.

Somewhere in this world is
YOUR KIND OF PLACE.
That is the place that you'll slow down your pace.

You'll unpack your bags, you'll play and you'll stay.

You'll put off your travels for some other day.

Then some other day you'll be off on safari,
Where starry night skies are endlessy starry.
You'll walk and you'll ride and you'll run and you'll fly,
And your life will be better, as long as YOU TRY.

Your feet may get blisters.
Your shoes may wear through.
Your legs might give out,
As legs **SOMETIMES DO.**

Or you may be delayed when a storm comes your way,
Or your bag will go missing (now there's a dark day).
Or you may be too late, and you might miss your flight,
Or suffer from jet lag and **BE UP ALL NIGHT.**

Those things are just hiccups. Tomorrow you'll see.
You'll be back on your feet, you'll be good as can be.
Then onward and upward, ahead at full steam,
You'll make your dreams happen,
NO MATTER THE DREAM.

There are limitless wonders—you can't see them all.

The earth is too large, and you are too small.

When planning your plans, think them thoroughly through,

THEN GO WITH YOUR GUT—

it knows what to do.